MW01139389

It's Snot Fair!

(and other gross & disgusting jokes)

for Luke!
Brenda

It's not
Booger
Carnival
either!

Brenda Ponnay

Copyright © Brenda Ponnay 2017

All Rights Reserved. No portion of this book may be reproduced without
express permission from the publisher.
First Edition
ISBN-13: 978-1-53240-224-1
eISBN: 978-1-53240-225-8
Published in the United States by Xist Publishing
www.xistpublishing.com
PO Box 61593 Irvine, CA 92602

xist Publishing

It's Snot Fair!

(and other gross & disgusting jokes)

Brenda Ponnay

Why did the skeleton burp?

Because it didn't have the guts to fart.

Why don't snowmen eat carrot cake?

They're afraid it has boogers in it.

How do you make a tissue dance?

Put a little boogie in it.

Why did the girl take toilet paper to the party?

Because she's a party pooper.

What do you call a fly without wings?

A walk!

What's invisible and smells like carrots?

Bunny Farts!

What's yellow and gooey and smells like bananas?

Monkey snot.

Why do gorillas have large nostrils?

Because they have fat fingers.

Why did the toad cross the road?

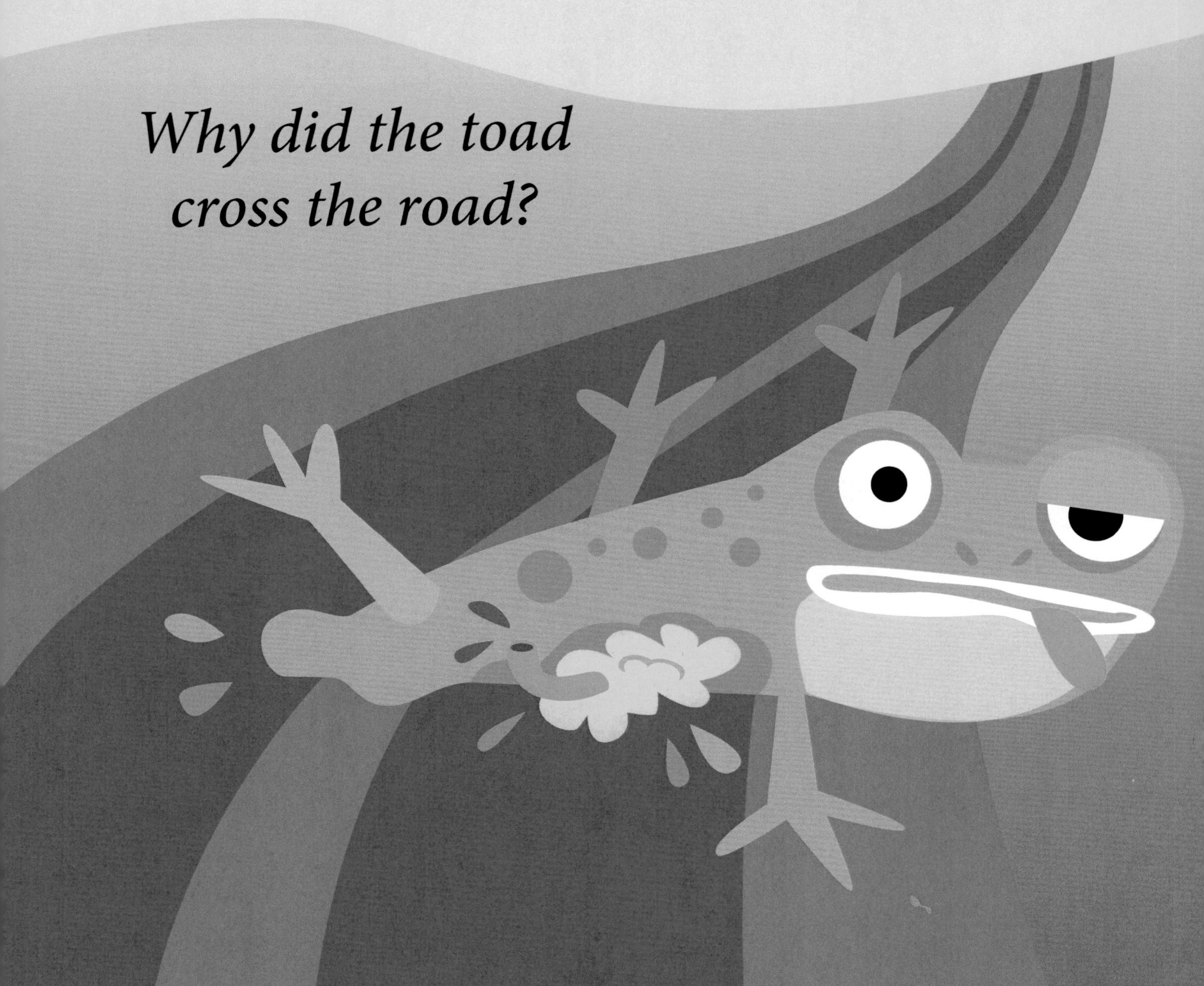

To show his friends that he has GUTS!

What did one toilet say to the other toilet?

You look a bit flushed.

How does a kid take a bubble bath when he's out of bubble bath soap?

He eats beans for dinner.

Why should you only put 239 beans in bean soup?

Cuz one more will make it "too farty!"

What happened when the chef found a daddy long legs in the salad?
It became a daddy short legs!

What does an elephant keep up its trunk?

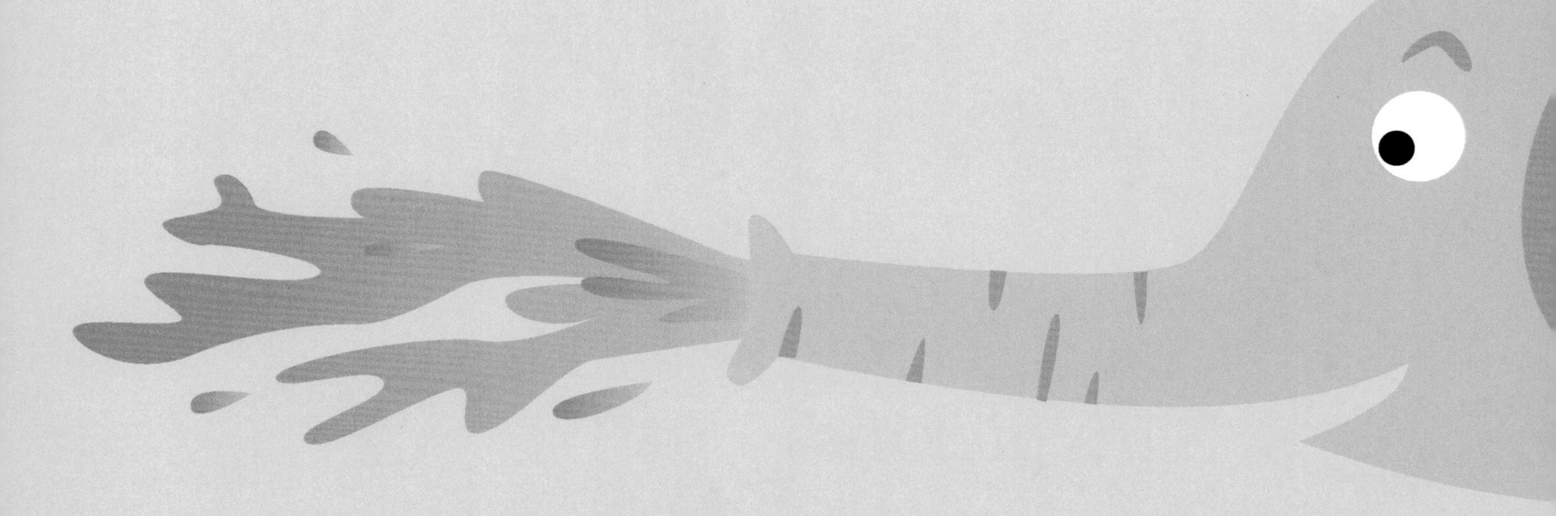

A yard and a half of snot!

What do you call a skinny booger?

Slim pickins.

What does a booger tell his girlfriend?

I’m stuck
on you.

What do you get when the Queen farts?

A noble gas.

What's another name for a snail?

A booger with a crash helmet.

What did the baby slime say to its mommy?

Goo-goo!

What is worse than finding a worm in your apple?

Finding half a worm!

How do you make a glow worm happy?

Cut off his tail, he'll be de-lighted!

What do you call it when evil worms take over the world?

Global Worming!

What do you call a dinosaur that does not take a bath?

A Stink-o-Saurus.

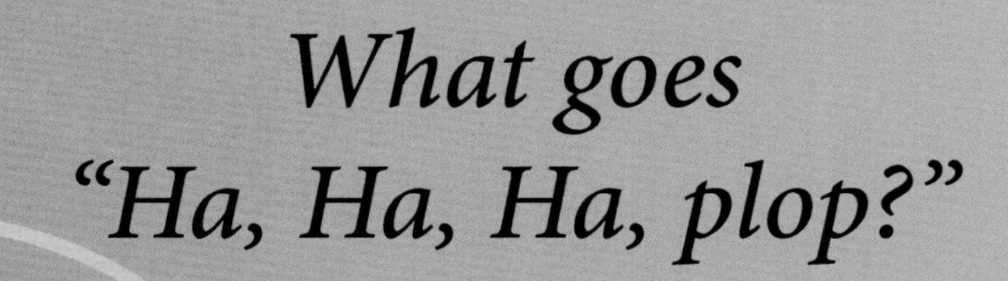

What goes
"Ha, Ha, Ha, plop?"

Haha
haha
ha HA!
haha
ha HAH!

Someone laughing their head off.

What color is a burp?

Burple.

What did one burp say to the other burp?

"Let's be stinkers and go out the other end!"

What do you call a bear with no teeth?

A gummy bear!

What's yellow and lumpy and smells like a zebra?

Lion puke!

Hey kids,
Please be kind to your
parents and only read
this book aloud once...
or maybe twice.

About the Author

Brenda Ponnay is the author and illustrator of several children's books including the Secret Agent Josephine series, the Little Hoo series, the Time for Bunny series and an on-going series of joke books. She lives in Southern California with her family who inspire her daily.

You can read all about their adventures on her personal blog www.secret-agent-josephine.com

73353667R00020

Made in the USA
Columbia, SC
10 July 2017